HENRY EVERY : STORY OF A PIRATE WHO ROBBED MUGHAL TREASURE

GOLU KUMAR

Contents

ONE

Avery was the most talked-about of these daring explorers for a time; he made as much noise in the world as Meriveis does now and was regarded as a person of equal importance. He was portrayed in Europe as having attained the dignity of a king and was likely to be the founder of a new monarchy; he was said to have amassed enormous wealth and married the Great Mogul's daughter, who was abducted by an Indian ship. which came into his hands, and that he had many children by her, living in great royalty and state; that he had built forts, erected magazines, and was the master of a strong squadron of ships, manned with capable and desperate fellows of all Nations; that he issued commissions in his name to the captains of his ships, and the commanders of his forts, and was recognized by them as their Prince. He was the subject of a play titled "The Successful Pyrate," and these accounts gained such notoriety that the Council received multiple proposals for setting up a squadron to capture him. Others, however, advocated for extending an act of grace to him and his companions and welcoming them to England with all of their wealth lest his rising Greatness impedes trade from Europe to the East Indies.

However, all of these were nothing more than untrue rumors that were made more credible by the credulity of some and the wit of others who enjoy making up strange stories. For example, while it was claimed that he was aspiring for a Crown, he wanted a Shilling, and at the same time that it was claimed he had such extraordinary wealth in Madagascar, he was going hungry in England.

Without a doubt, the reader will be curious to learn what happened to this man and what the real reasons were for so many erroneous reports about him; as a result, I will provide his history in as few words as I can.

He was born in the West of _England_ near _Plymouth_ in _Devonshire_, being bred to the Sea, he served as a Mate of a Merchant-Man, in several trading Voyages: It happened before the Peace of _Ryfwick_ when there was an Alliance betwixt _Spain_, _England_, _Holland_, _&c._ against _France_, that the _French_ in _Martinico_, carried on a smuggling Trade with the _Spaniards_ on the Continent of _Peru_, which by the Laws of _Spain_, is not allowed to Friends in Time of Peace, for none but native _Spaniards_ are permitted to Traffick in those Parts, or set their Feet on Shore unless at any time they are brought as Prisoners; wherefore they constantly keep certain Ships cruising along the Coast, whom they call _Guarda del Costa_, who have the Orders to make Prizes of all ships they can light of within five Leagues of Land. Now the _French_ growing very bold in Trade, and the _Spaniards_ being poorly provided with Ships, and those they had being of no Force, it often fell out, that when the light of the _French_ Smugglers, they were not strong enough to attack them, therefore it was resolv'd in _Spain_, to hire two or three stout foreign Ships for their Service, which knowing at _Bristol_, some Merchants of that City, fitted out two Ships of thirty odd Guns, and 120 Hands each, well furnished with Provision and Ammunition, and all other Stores; and the

Hire being agreed for, by some Agents for _Spain_, they were commanded to sail for _Corunna_ or the _Groine_, there to receive their Orders, and to take on Board some _Spanish_ Gentlemen, who were to go Passengers to _New-Spain_.

Of one of these Ships, which I take to be called the _Duke_, Capt. _Gibson_ Commander, _Avery_ was the first Mate, and being a Fellow of more Cunning than Courage, he insinuated himself into the good Will of several of the boldest Fellows on Board the other Ship, as well as that which he was on Board of; having sounded their Inclinations before he opened himself, and finding them ripe for his Design, he, at length, proposed to them, to run away with the Ship, telling them what great Wealth was to be had upon the Coasts of _India_. It was no sooner said than agreed to, and they resolved to execute their Plot at Ten Clock the Night following.

It must be observ'd, the Captain was one of those who are mightily addicted to Punch, so that he passed most of his time on Shore, in some little drinking Ordinary; but this Day he did not go on Shore as usual; however, this did not spoil the Design, for he took his usual Dose on Board, and so got to Bed before the Hour appointed for the Business: The Men also who were not privy to the Design, turned into their Hammocks, leaving none upon Deck but the Conspirators, who, indeed, were the greatest Part of the Ship's Crew. At the time agreed on, the _Dutchess_'s Longboat appear'd, which _Avery_ hailing in the usual manner, was answered by the Men in her, _Is your drunken Boatswain on Board?_ Which was the Watch-Word agreed between them, and _Avery_ replying in the Affirmative, the Boat came aboard with sixteen stout Fellows and joined the Company.

When our Gentry saw that all was clear, they secured
the Hatches, so went to work; they did not slip the Anchor,
but weigh'd it leisurely, and so put to Sea without any
Disorder or Confusion, tho' there were several Ships then
lying in the Bay, and among them, a _Dutch_ Frigate of forty
Guns, the Captain of which was offered a great Reward to go
out after her; but _Mynheer_, who perhaps would not have
been willing to have been served so himself could not be
prevailed upon to give such Usage to another, and so let Mr.
Avery pursue his Voyage, whither he had a Mind to.

The Captain, who by this time, was awaked, either by
the Motion of the Ship, or the Noise of working the Tackles,
rung the Bell; _Avery_ and two others went into the Cabin;
the Captain, half asleep, and in a kind of Fright, ask'd,
What was the Matter? _Avery_ answered cooly,
Nothing; the Captain replied, _something's the Matter
with the Ship, Does she drive? What Weather is it?_
Thinking nothing less than that it had been a Storm, and
that the Ship was driven from her Anchors: _No, no_,
answered _Avery_, _we're at Sea, with a fair Wind and good
Weather. At Sea! _says the Captain, _How can that be?
Come_, says _Avery, don't be in a Fright but put on your
Cloaths, and I'll let you into a Secret: -- You must know,
that I am Captain of this Ship now, and this is my Cabin,
therefore you must walk out; I am bound to _Madagascar_,
with a Design of making my Fortune, and that of all the
brave Fellows joined with me._

The Captain had a little recovered his Senses, began to
apprehend the meaning; however, his Fright was as great
as before, which _Avery_ perceiving, bad him fear nothing,
for, says he, if you have a Mind to make one of us, we
will receive you, and if you'll turn sober, and mind your
Business, perhaps in Time I may make you one of my

Lieutenants, if not, here's a Boat a-long-side, and you shall be set ashore.

The Captain was glad to hear this, and therefore accepted of his Offer, and the whole Crew being called up, to know who was willing to go on Shore with the Captain, and who to seek their Fortunes with the rest; there were not above five or six who were willing to quit this Enterprize; wherefore they were put into the Boat with the Captain that Minute and made their Way to the Shore as well as they could.

They proceeded on their Voyage to _Madagascar_, but I do not find they took any Ships in their Way; when they arrived at the N. E. Part of that Island, they found two Sloops at Anchor, who, upon seeing them, slip'd their Cables and run themselves ashore, the Men all landing, and running into the Woods; these were two Sloops which the Men had run away with from the _West-Indies_, and seeing _Avery_, they supposed him to be some Frigate sent to take them, and therefore not being of Force to engage him, they did what they could to save themselves.

He guessed where they were, and sent some of his Men on Shore to let them know they were Friends, and to offer they might join together for their common Safety; the Sloops Men were well armed and had posted themselves in a Wood, with Centinels just on the outside, to observe whether the Ship landed her Men to pursue them, and they observing only two or three men come towards them without Arms, did not oppose them, but has challenged them, and they answering they were Friends, they lead them to their Body, where they delivered their Message; at first, they apprehended it was a Stratagem to decoy them on Board, but when the Ambassadors offered that the Captain himself, and as many of the Crew as they should name, would meet them on Shore without Arms, they believed them to be in Earnest, and they soon entered into a Confidence with one another; those on Board going on Shore, and some of those on Shore going on Board.

The Sloops Men were rejoiced at the new Ally, for their Vessels were so small, that they could not attack a Ship of any Force so that hitherto they had not taken any considerable Prize, but now they hoped to fly at high Game; and _Avery_ was as well pleased with this Reinforcement, to strengthen them, for any brave Enterprize, and tho' the Booty must be lessened to each, by being divided into so many Shares, yet he found out an Expedient not to suffer by it himself as shall be shown in its Place.

Having consulted what was to be done, they resolved to sail out together upon a Cruize, the Galley and two Sloops; they therefore fell to work to get the Sloops off, which they soon effected, and steered towards the _Arabian_ Coast; near the River _Indus_, the Man at the Mast-Head spied a Sail, upon which they gave Chace, and as they came nearer to her, they perceived her to be a tall Ship, and fancied she might be a _Dutch East-India_ Man homeward bound; but she proved a better Prize; when they fired at her to bring too, she hoisted _Mogul_'s Colours, and seemed to stand upon her Defence; _Avery_ only canonaded at a Distance, and some of his Men began to suspect that he was not the Hero they took him for: However, the Sloops made Use of their Time, and coming one on the Bow, and the other on the Quarter, of the Ship, clapt her on Board, and enter'd her, upon which she immediately struck her Colours and yielded; she was one of the _Great Mogul_'s own Ships, and there were in her several of the greatest Persons of his Court, among whom it was said was one of his Daughters, who were going on a Pilgrimage to _Mecca_, the

Mahometans thinking themselves obliged once in their Lives to visit that Place, and they were carrying with them rich Offerings to present at the Shrine of _Mahomet_. It is known that the Eastern People travel with the utmost Magnificence so that they had with them all their Slaves and Attendants, their rich Habits and Jewels, Vessels of Gold and Silver, and great Sums of Money to defray the Charges of their Journey by Land; wherefore the Plunder got by this Prize, is not easily computed.

Having taken all the Treasure on Board their Ships, and plundered their Prize of every Thing else they either wanted or liked, they let her go; she not being able to continue her Voyage, returned: As soon as the News came to the _Mogul_, and he knew that they were _English_ who had robbed them, he threatened loud and talked of sending a mighty Army with Fire and Sword, to extirpate the _English_ from all their Settlements on the _Indian_ Coast. The _East-India_ Company in _England_were very much alarmed at it; however, by Degrees, they found Means to pacify him, by promising to do their Endeavours to take the Robbers, and deliver them into his hands; however, the great Noise this Thing made in Europe, as well as _India_, was the Occasion of all these romantic Stories which were formed of _Avery_'s Greatness.

In the meantime, our successful Plunderers agreed to make the best of their Way back to _Madagascar_, intending to make that place their Magazine or Repository for all their Treasure, and to build a small Fortification there, and leave a few Hands always ashore to look after it, and defend it from any Attempts of the Natives; but _Avery_ put an End to this Project, and made it altogether unnecessary.

As they were Steering their Course, as has been said, he sends a Boat on Board of each of the Sloops, desiring the Chief of them to come on Board of him, in order to hold a Council; they did so, and he told them he had something to propose to them for the common Good, which was to provide against Accidents; he bad them consider the Treasure they were possess'd of, would be sufficient for them all if they could secure it in some Place on Shore; therefore all they had to fear, was some Misfortune in the Voyage; he bad them consider the Consequences of being separated by bad Weather, in which Case, the Sloops, if either of them should fall in with any Ships of Force, must be either taken or sunk, and the Treasure on Board her lost to the rest, besides the common Accidents of the Sea; as for his Part he was so strong, he was able to make his Party good with any Ship they were like to meet in those Seas; that if he met with any Ship of such Strength, that he could not take her, he was safe from being taken, being so well mann'd; besides his Ship was a quick Sailor, and could carry Sail, when the Sloops could not, wherefore, he proposed to them, to put the Treasure on Board his Ship, to seal up each Chest with 3 Seals, whereof each was to keep one, and to appoint a Rendezvous, in Case of Separation.

Upon considering this Proposal, it appeared so seasonable to them, that they readily came into it, for they argued to themselves, that an Accident might happen to one of the Sloops and the other escape, wherefore it was for the common Good. The Thing was done as agreed to, the Treasure put on Board of _Avery_, and the Chests seal'd; they kept Company that Day and the next, the Weather being fair, in which Time _Avery_ tampered with his Men, telling them they now had sufficient, to make them all easy, and what should hinder them from going to some Country, where they were not known, and living on Shore all the rest of their Days in Plenty; they understood what he meant: And in short, they all agreed to bilk their new Allies, the Sloop's Men, nor do I find that any of them felt any Qualms of Honour rising in his Stomach, to hinder them from consenting to this Piece of Treachery. In fine, they took advantage of the Darkness that Night, steered another Course, and, by Morning, lost Sight of them.

I leave the Reader to judge, what Swearing and Confusion there was among the Sloop's Men, in the Morning when they saw that _Avery_ had given them the Slip; for they knew by the Fairness of the Weather, and the Course they had agreed to steer, that it must have been done on purpose: But we leave them at present to follow Mr. _Avery_.

Avery, and his Men, having consulted what to do with themselves, came to a Resolution, to make the best of their Way towards _America_; and none of them being known in those Parts, they intended to divide the Treasure, to change their Names, to go ashore, some in one Place, some in other, to purchase some Settlements, and live at Ease. The first Land they made, was the Island of _Providence_, then newly settled; here they stayed some Time, and having considered that when they should go to _New-England_, the Greatness of their Ship, would cause much Enquiry about them; and possibly some People from _England_, who had heard the Story of a Ship's being run away with from the _Groine_, might suspect them to be the People; they, therefore, took a Resolution of disposing of their Ship at _Providence_: Upon which, _Avery_ pretending that the Ship being fitted out upon the privateering Account, and having had no Success, he had received Orders from the Owners, to dispose of her to the best Advantage, he soon met with a Purchaser, and immediately bought a sloop.

In this Sloop, he and his Companions embarked, they touched at several Parts of _America_, where no Person suspected them; and some of them went on Shore, and dispersed themselves about the Country, having received such Dividends as _Avery_ would give them; for he concealed the greatest Part of the Diamonds from them, which in the first Hurry of plundering the Ship, they did not much regard, as not knowing their Value.

Finally, he arrived in Boston, New England, and appeared to be considering settling there; some of his companions even went ashore; however, he later changed his mind and suggested that the few companions that were still with him set sail for Ireland. He realized that New England was not the best location for him because a large portion of his wealth was in diamonds, and should he have produced them there, he would have undoubtedly been better off.

In their Voyage to Ireland, they avoided St. _George_'s Channel, and sailing North about, they put into one of the Northern Ports of that Kingdom; there they disposed of their Sloop and coming on Shore they separated themselves, some going to _Cork_, and some to _Dublin_, 18 of whom obtained their Pardons afterward of K. _William_. When _Avery_ had remain'd some Time in this Kingdom, he was afraid to offer his Diamonds to sale, least an Enquiry into his Manner of coming by them should occasion a Discovery; therefore considering with himself what was best to be done, he fancied there were some Persons at _Bristol_, whom he might venture to trust; upon which, he resolved to pass over into _England_; he did so, and going into _Devonshire_, he sent to one of these Friends to meet him at a Town called _Biddiford_; when he had communicated himself to his Friends, and consulted with him about the Means of his Effects, they agreed, that the safest Method would be, to put them in the Hands of some Merchants, who being Men of Wealth and Credit in the World, no Enquiry would be made how they came by them; this Friend telling him he was very intimate with some who were very fit for the Purpose, and if he would but allow them a good Commission would do the Business very faithfully. _Avery_ liked the Proposal, for he found no other Way of managing his Affairs since he could not appear in them himself; therefore his Friend went back to _Bristol_, and opened the Matter to the Merchants, they made _Avery_ a Visit at _Biddiford_, where, after some Protestations of Honour and Integrity, he delivered them his Effects, consisting of Diamonds and some Vessels of Gold; they gave him a little money for his present Subsistence, and so they parted.

He changed his name and lived at _Biddiford_, without making any Figure, and therefore there was no great Notice taken of him; yet let one or two of his Relations know where he was, who came to see him. In some time his little Money was spent, yet he heard nothing from his Merchants; he writ to them often, and after many importunities, they sent him a small Supply, but scarcely sufficient to pay his Debts: In fine, the Supplies they sent him from Time to Time, were so small, that they were not sufficient to give him Bread, nor could he get that little, without a great deal of Trouble and Importunity, wherefore being weary of his life, he went privately to _Bristol_, to speak to the Merchants himself, where instead of Money he met a most shocking Repulse, for when he desired them to come to an Account with him, they silenced him by threatening to discover him so that our Merchants were as good Pyrates at Land as he was at

Sea.

Whether he was frightened by these Menaces or had seen some Body else he thought knew him, is not known; but he went immediately over to _Ireland_, and from thence solicited his Merchants very hard for a Supply, but to no Purpose, for he was even reduced to beggary: In this Extremity, he was resolved to return and cast himself upon them, let the Consequence be what it would. He put himself on Board a trading Vessel, and worked his Passage over to _Plymouth_, from whence he traveled on Foot to _Biddiford_, where he had been but a few days before he fell sick and died; not being worth as much as would buy him a Coffin.

This is all the information I could find about this man, dismissing the untrue stories that were told about his improbable greatness, according to which his deeds were less significant than those of other pirates even though he caused more noise in the world.

We will now go back and tell our readers what happened to the two Sloops.

We took Notice of the Rage and Confusion, which must have seized them, upon their missing of _Avery_; however, they continued their Course, some of them still flattering themselves that he had only out sailed them in the Night and that they should find him at the Place of Rendezvous: But when they came there and could hear no Tydings of him, there was an End of Hope. It was time to consider what they should do with themselves, their Stock of Sea Provision was almost spent, and tho' there was Rice and Fish, and Fowl to be had ashore, these would not keep for Sea, without being properly cured with Salt, which they had no Convenience of doing; therefore, since they could not go a Cruizing any more, it was time to think of establishing themselves at Land; to which Purpose they took all Things out of the Sloops, made Tents of the Sails, and encamped themselves, having a large Quantity of Ammunition, and abundance of small Arms.

Since this will only be a little digression, we shall describe how they arrived at this location where they encountered some of their fellow countrymen who were part of the crew of a privateer sloop under the command of Captain Thomas Tew.

Captain _George Dew_ and Captain _Thomas Tew_, having received Commissions from the then Governor of _Bermudas_, sail directly for the River _the Gambia_ in _Africa_; there, with the Advice and Assistance of the Agents of the Royal _African_ Company, they to attempt the taking the _French_ Factory at _Goorie_, lying upon that Coast. In a few days after they sailed out, _Dew_ in a violent Storm, not only sprung his Mast, but lost Sight of his Consort; _Dew_, therefore, returned to refit, and _Tew_ instead of proceeding on his Voyage, made for the _Cape of Good Hope_, and doubling the said Cape, shaped his Course for the Straits of _Babel Mandel_, being the Entrance into the _Red Sea_. Here he came up with a large Ship, richly laden, bound from the _Indies_ to _Arabia_, with three hundred Soldiers on Board, besides Seamen; yet _Tew_ had the Hardiness to board her, and soon carried her; and, 'tis said, by this Prize, his Men shared near three thousand Pounds a Piece: They had Intelligence from the Prisoners, of five other rich Ships to pass that Way, which _Tew_ would have attacked, tho' they were very strong, if he had not been over-ruled by the Quarter-Master and others.--This differing in Opinion created some ill Blood amongst them so that they resolved to break up pirating, and no place was so fit to receive them as _Madagascar_; hither they steered, resolving to live on Shore and enjoy what they got.

As for Tew, he soon traveled to Rhode Island with a small group of people and there made peace.

We have now explained the company that our pirates encountered in this location.

It must be observed that the Natives of _Madagascar_ are a kind of Negroes, they differ from those of _Guiney_ in their Hair, which is long, and their Complexion is not so good a Jet; they have innumerable little Princes among them, who are continually making War upon one another; their Prisoners are their Slaves, and they either sell them, or put them to death, as they please: When our Pyrates first settled amongst them, their Alliance was much courted by these Princes, so they sometimes joined one, sometimes another, but wheresoever they sided, they were sure to be Victorious; for the Negroes here had no Fire-Arms, nor did they understand their Use; so that at length these Pyrates became so terrible to the Negroes, that if two or three of them were only seen on one side when they were going to engage, the opposite side would fly without striking a Blow.

By these means they not only became feared, but powerful; all the Prisoners of War, they took to be their Slaves; they married the most beautiful of the Negroe Women; not one or two, but as many as they liked; so that every one of them had as great a Seraglio as the Grand Seignior at _Constantinople_: The Slaves they employed in planting Rice, in Fishing, Hunting, _&c._ besides which, they had an abundance of others, who lived, as it were, under their Protection, and to be secure from the Disturbances or Attacks of their powerful Neighbours; these seemed to pay them a willing Homage. Now they began to divide from one another, each living with his Wives, Slaves, and Dependants, like a separate Prince; and as Power and Plenty naturally beget Contention, they sometimes quarreled with one another, and attacked each other at the Head of their several Armies; and in these civil Wars, many of them were killed; but an Accident happened, which obliged them to unite again for their common Safety.

It must be observed that these sudden great Men, had used their Power like Tyrants, for they grew wanton in Cruelty, and nothing was more common than upon the slightest Displeasure, to cause one of their Dependants to be tied to a Tree and shot thro' the Heart, let the Crime be what it would, whether little or great, this was always the Punishment; wherefore the Negroes conspired together, to rid themselves of these Destroyers, all in one Night; and as they now lived separate, the Thing might easily have been done, had not a Woman, who had been Wife or Concubine to one of them, run near twenty Miles in three Hours, to discover the Matter to them: Immediately upon the Alarm they ran together as fast as they could so that when the Negroes approached them, they found them all up in Arms; wherefore they retired without making any Attempt.

It will be worthwhile to discuss the policy of these rude fellows and to show what measures they did to secure themselves because this Escape made them very careful from that point on.

They found that the Fear of their Power could not secure them against a Surprize, and the bravest Man may be killed when he is asleep, by one much his inferior in Courage and Strength, therefore, as their first Security, they did all they could to foment War betwixt the neighboring Negroes, remaining Neuter themselves, by which Means, those who were overcome constantly lied to them for Protection, otherwise, they must be either killed or made Slaves. They strengthened their Party, and tied some to them by interest;

when there was no War, they contrived to spirit up private Quarrels among them, and upon every little Dispute or Misunderstanding, push on one side or other to Revenge; instruct them how to attack or surprise their Adversaries, and lend them loaded Pistols or Firelocks to dispatch them with; the Consequence of which was, that the Murderer was forced to fly to them for the safety of his Life, with his Wives, Children, and Kindred.

Such as these were fast Friends, as their lives depended upon the safety of his Protectors; for as we observed before, our Pyrates were grown so terrible, that none of their Neighbours had Resolution enough to attack them in an open War.

By such Arts as these, in the Space of a few years, their Body was greatly increased, they then began to separate themselves, and remove at a greater Distance from one another, for the Convenience of more Ground, and were divided like Jews, into Tribes, each carrying with him his Wives and Children, (of which, by this time they had a large Family,) as also their Quota of Dependants and Followers; and if Power and Command be the Thing which distinguishes a Prince, these Ruffians had all the Marks of Royalty about them, nay more, they had the very Fears which commonly disturb Tyrants, as may be seen by the extreme Caution they took in fortifying the Places where they dwelt.

In this Plan of Fortification they imitated one another, their Dwellings were rather Citadels than Houses; they made Choice of a Place overgrown with Wood, and scituate near a Water; they raised a Rampart or high Ditch round it, so strait and high, that it was impossible to climb it, and especially by those who had not the Use of scaling Ladders: Over this Ditch there was one Passage into the Wood; the

Dwelling, which was a Hut, was built in that Part of the Wood which the Prince, who inhabited it, thought fit, but so covered that it could not be seen till you came at it; but the greatest Cunning lay in the Passage which lead to the Hut, which was so narrow, that no more than one Person could go a Breast, and contrived in so intricate a Manner, that it was a perfect Maze or Labyrinth, it being round and round, with several little cross Ways, so that a Person that was not well acquainted with the Way, might walk several Hours round and cross these Ways without being able to find the Hut; moreover all along the Sides of these narrow Paths, certain large Thorns which grew upon a Tree in that Country, were struck into the Ground with their Points uppermost, and the Path it self being made crooked and serpentine, if a Man should attempt to come near the Hut at Night, he would certainly have struck upon these Thorns, tho' he had been provided with that Clue which _Ariadne_ gave to _Theseus_ when he entered the Cave of the _Minataur_.

Thus Tyrant like they lived, fearing and feared by all; and in this situation, they were found by Captain _Woods Rogers_, when he went to _Madagascar_, in the _Delicia_, a Ship of forty Guns, with a Design of buying Slaves to sell to the _Dutch_ at _Batavia_ or _New-Holland_: He happened to touch upon a Part of the Island, where no Ship had been seen for seven or eight Years before, where he met with some of the Pyrates, at which time, they had been upon the Island above 25 Years, having a large mostly Generation of Children and Grand-Children descended from them, there being about that Time, eleven of them remaining alive.

Upon their first seeing a Ship of this Force and Burthen, they supposed it to be a Man of War sent to take them; they, therefore, lurked within their Fastnesses, but when some from the Ship came on Shore, without any shew of Hostility, and offering to trade with the Negroes, they ventured to come out of their Holes, attended like Princes; and since they are Kings _De Facto_, which is a kind of a Right, we ought to speak of them as such.

Having been so many Years upon this Island, it may be imagined, their Cloaths had long been worn out, so that their Majesties were extremely out at the Elbows; I cannot say they were ragged, since they had no Cloaths, they had nothing to cover them but the Skins of Beasts without any tanning, but with all the Hair on, nor a Shoe nor Stocking, so they looked like the Pictures of _Hercules_ in Lion's Skin; and being overgrown with Beard, and Hair upon their Bodies, they appeared the most savage Figures that a Man's Imagination can frame.

However, they soon got rigg'd, for they sold great Numbers of those poor People under them, for Cloaths, Knives, Saws, Powder and Ball, and many other things, and became so familiar that they went aboard the _Delicia_, and were observed to be very curious, examining the inside of the Ship, and very familiar with the Men, inviting them ashore. Their Design in doing this, as they afterwards confessed, was to try if it was not practicable to surprize the Ship in the Night, which they judged very easy, in case there was but a slender Watch kept on Board, they having Boats and Men enough at Command, but it seems the Captain was aware of them, and kept so strong a Watch upon Deck, that they found it was in vain to make any Attempt; wherefore, when some of the Men went ashore, they were for inveigling them, and drawing them into a Plot, for seizing the Captain and securing the rest of the Men under Hatches, when they should have the Night-Watch, promising a Signal to come on Board to join them;

proposing, if they succeeded, to go a Pyrating together, not doubting but with that Ship they should be able to take any Thing they met on the Sea: But the Captain observing an intimacy growing betwixt them and some of his Men, thought it could be for no good, he therefore broke it off in Time, not suffering them so much as to talk together; and when he sent a Boat on Shore with an Officer to treat with them about the Sale of Slaves, the Crew remained on Board the Boat, and no Man was suffered to talk with them, but the Person deputed by him for that Purpose.

They confessed all of their plans to harm him before he set to ship and threalizedsed there was nothing they could do. As a result, he left them in the same state and position that he had discovered them in—a very filthy State and Royalty—but with fewer subjects than they had, having, as we saw, sold many of them. If Ambition is the dearest passion of Men, then they were undoubtedly content. One of these great princes had previously worked as a waterman on the Thames, where he committed a murder and fled to the West Indies, joining the ranks of those who escaped with the schooners. The other men had all beforecastedted, and there was not a single man among them who could read or write, yet their secretaries of state had no more education than they did. This is the only account we have of these Kings of Madagascar, some of whom are likely still in power today.